D0442618

Alice's Birthday Pig

Alice's Birthday Pig

Written by

Tim Kennemore

Illustrated by

Mike Spoor

EERDMANS BOOKS FOR YOUNG READERS
GRAND RAPIDS, MICHIGAN / CAMBRIDGE, U.K.

Text © 2005 Tim Kennemore
Illustrations © 2005 Mike Spoor
All rights reserved

First published 2005 by Andersen Press Ltd,
20 Vauxhall Bridge Road
London SW1V 2SA, England

This edition published 2008 by
Eerdmans Books for Young Readers,
an imprint of Wm. B. Eerdmans Publishing Co.

Wm. B. Eerdmans Publishing Co.
2140 Oak Industrial Dr. N.E., Grand Rapids, Michigan 49505
P.O. Box 163, Cambridge CB3 9PU U.K.
www.eerdmans.com/youngreaders

Printed in the United States of America

08 09 10 11 12   8 7 6 5 4 3 2 1

Library of Congress Cataloging-in-Publication Data

Kennemore, Tim.
Alice's birthday pig / written by Tim Kennemore; illustrated by Mike Spoor.
p.   cm.
Summary: Alice's brother teases her mercilessly because she cannot say the word
"animal" correctly, but she gets her revenge on her birthday.
ISBN 978-0-8028-5335-6 (hardcover: alk. paper)
[1. Family life — Fiction. 2. Brothers and sisters — Fiction.]
I. Spoor, Mike, ill. II. Title.
PZ7.K392Al 2008
[E] — dc22

2007025460

Text type set in Lexicon

For Tom

Contents

1

Don't Feed the Aminals

For some time after Alice Singer learned to talk properly there was still one word that never seemed to come out right when she tried to say it.

That word was *animal*.

However hard Alice tried, what she always said was *aminal*.

It always came out the wrong way. She didn't know how it happened. She knew what she wanted to say, but it seemed to turn inside out somewhere between her brain and her mouth. Alice practiced and practiced saying it right. She tried saying it very quickly, before it had a chance to play tricks on her. She tried building herself up for it with a huge, long think. Nothing made any difference. She even tried standing on her head to see if saying it upside down would help.

"Aminal!" she said, and fell over.

It was hopeless.

Alice's brother Oliver teased her about it. "You talk just the same as Rosie," he said. "You're really such a baby still, Alice."

This made Alice absolutely furious. Rosie, their little sister, was only three, and said hundreds of words wrong. She talked complete nonsense most of the time. And Alice only had trouble with one tiny word in the whole wide world. It wasn't fair.

The best thing, Alice thought, was to try not to say the word at all and hope the problem worked itself out as she grew older. She was managing this quite well, until the day she went back to school after Easter vacation and her teacher, Miss Jones, said, "I know you're all wondering what your class topic is going to be this semester!"

Alice sat up straight and listened. Last semester their topic had been "Canals and Rivers," and

they'd had an amazing canal boat trip as their special class field trip.

"Would anyone like to guess?" asked Miss Jones.

"I do, I do," said Danny Tolliver, waving his hand in the air.

Miss Jones looked at him suspiciously. Any contribution from Danny Tolliver usually meant trouble.

"Yes, Danny?"

"Spiders and snakes!" said Danny.

Some of the stupid girls, like Rebecca Richards, squealed and shuddered and said "Ugh!" Alice glared at them. Anyone would think Danny Tolliver had pulled handfuls of wriggling worms out of his pocket and thrown them around the room, the fuss those girls made.

Miss Jones sighed. "No, Danny. We are not doing spiders and snakes. In fact we won't be touching on insects or reptiles of any sort whatever. Neither are we doing vampires, ghosts, werewolves, slimy blobby things . . . "

"Oh, I know!" Up went the hand of Jamie

Logan, who was Danny Tolliver's best friend. Jamie Logan had a pet rat called Semesterinator.

"No, I don't think we'll have any more guesses, thank you," said Miss Jones, looking at him darkly. "Are you listening, everyone? Our class topic for this semester is going to be . . . farm animals!"

Alice could see nothing but trouble ahead.

*   *   *

Alice's parents were the kind of parents who liked to talk at dinner about what everyone had done that day. First they would ask Rosie what she had broken and who she had hit at Humpty Dumpty, which was the only daycare left in town that hadn't thrown her out. As Rosie had usually broken a lot of things and hit a great many people, this part of the conversation would take quite some time.

But then it would be Alice's turn.

"And what about you, Alice? What did you do at school today?"

"Oh, the usual lessons and stuff," mumbled Alice. Usually she liked talking about school, but this semester was totally different. She hoped that if she made everything sound really boring, her parents would move on to Oliver before she was in any danger of needing to use the dreaded word. Oliver hovered like an eagle waiting to pounce on its prey.

"What's your class topic this semester again, Alice?" he asked, with a sweet smile on his face. "I keep forgetting."

Alice knew that Oliver knew perfectly well what her class topic was. The semester was three weeks old now, and they had talked about it several times at the dinner table already.

But suddenly Alice felt that *this* was the time she would get it right. She remembered the sound and the feel of the word *animal*. She had heard it so often at school during the week already! She cleared her head of everything except the word *animal,* took a deep breath, concentrated with every cell of her brain, and said: *"FARM AMINALS!"*

Oliver burst out laughing. "You mean *animals*, Alice?" he said. "It's not such a difficult word. You really must learn to say it properly."

"Aminals!" said Rosie.

This made Alice feel even worse.

"No, it's *animals*," Oliver told Rosie, and Rosie, who didn't like people arguing with her, poured the remains of her chocolate and strawberry ice cream into his lap.

Sometimes Alice felt very fond of her little sister.

*   *   *

There seemed to be no end to it. Alice could *not* say the word. Sometimes on her own in bed she could whisper it right the fourth or fifth time. But in real life you never got a fifth try. Oliver never even let you have a second try.

Mom and Dad could see how bad she felt. One day at dinner, Dad said, "Oliver, you must stop teasing Alice. When you were little you couldn't say *animal* properly either."

"I could too!"

"No, you couldn't," said Mom. "In fact, I've never known a child that could say that word right at first. Everyone starts out saying it the wrong way."

Suddenly Alice had an idea. "Well, then," she said, "I'll tell you what they should do. They should change it around and really call them 'aminals.' Then everyone would be born knowing the word right."

Oliver sniffed scornfully. Oliver had a pointy little nose that always looked like it was sniffing scornfully even when it wasn't. He was tall and thin, and liked to look downwards at people.

"Don't be ridiculous, Alice," he said. "They'd have to change every single dictionary and encyclopedia in the world. Every book anywhere that used the word *animal* would have to be torn to pieces and they'd have to make another one. Just because *you* can't say a word properly." Oliver thought that it was very important to be proper.

"And they'd have to change all the signs at the

zoo to say 'Don't Feed the Aminals,'" Mom said with a smile.

"And all the grown-ups would have to learn to say *aminal*," said Dad. "I bet they've all forgotten how."

Alice nodded thoughtfully. They probably had.

2

Triceratops

As the semester went by Alice became wiser. She learned that there were ways to get by without ever saying *animal*. She began to use the words "creatures" and "livestock" and "wild beasts" a great deal. Oliver tried and tried to catch her, but she was too quick for him.

In the second half of the semester her class had their outing to a farm. They had a fantastic day. It was even better than the canal trip. They all took notebooks and pencils, because they were supposed to write down things about the animals they saw.

But hardly anybody wrote a single word, because when you go to a farm, the last thing you want to do is to write. You just want to pet and feed the animals. Alice fell in love with a little pig with a bad leg, which limped around after her and rolled over for her to scratch its tummy.

Danny Tolliver chased a turkey around and around, shouting that he was going to have it stuffed for his Thanksgiving dinner, when all of a sudden the turkey stood still, turned around, and pecked a big chunk out of his hand. Blood poured out everywhere. Danny had to go to the hospital, and he missed the special farmhouse meal.

Alice thought this was very sensible of the turkey, and went back to give it the very last handful from her bag of animal feed, which she had been saving for her little pig. She stood a long way away from the turkey, and threw the food towards it. She felt quite nervous about this, and was ready to run for her life in case the turkey thought she was a friend of Danny Tolliver's. But the turkey ignored the food, probably because it was still chewing bits of Danny, and stalked away making satisfied gobbling noises. This was something of a relief.

Alice fetched the three-legged pig and plopped it down in the middle of the food, where it snorted and grunted and gobbled, collapsed on its back and wiggled its legs at Alice as if it hadn't even noticed that she'd given the food to the turkey first. Alice sighed. What a forgiving pig. A generous pig!

"I wish I could take you home with me," she said sadly, and for a moment she could have sworn she saw the pig wink.

*   *   *

"So how was your class outing, Alice?" asked Oliver that evening. "What did you see at the farm?"

Alice was ready for him. She wasn't even close to needing to use the word *animal*.

"Chickens!" she said. Her mother winked at her. "Pigs and goats and sheep, cows and ponies, ducks and geese and a very clever turkey!"

"Why was the turkey so clever?" Dad asked.

Alice told the story. Everybody laughed, except Oliver. Then she told them about her little

14

lame pig. "It was so tame you wouldn't believe it, and it made such sweet little snuffly noises!"

"You make little snuffly noises when you've got a cold," said Mom, "and there's nothing sweet about it at all."

"Pigs are different," said Alice dreamily, gazing out of the window into the yard.

Their yard was quite big, but nobody much liked gardening so there was hardly anything out there — just a lot of long grass and a shed at the end. Suddenly she had a stunningly good idea. "Look at all that garden!"

"Pardon?" said Mom.

"Wasted!" said Alice. "Room to give a home to a poor unwanted . . . creature!"

"I'm not going to like this," said Dad.

"A pig would be just the thing!" said Alice. "I know! Let's buy that pig I saw today!"

"No," said Mom and Dad together.

"But I'm sure it's no good to them on the farm because of its leg, and we could give it such a good home!"

"No," said Mom and Dad together.

15

Alice tried desperately to think of good things that pigs provided, but all that came to mind were sausages. Pigs were their own worst enemies! Why, oh why didn't they make milk or lay eggs?

"I want a pig!" said Rosie, but nobody took any notice.

"Oliver's got a rabbit!" said Alice, starting to lose hope but not yet ready to give up.

"No," said Mom and Dad together.

"I'd look after it all by myself!" said Alice desperately.

"Would you now?" said Dad. "Would you go out there three times a day with your piggy scooper and pick up all the pig poo before Rosie got her hands on it?"

There was a long silence while everybody thought about what Rosie might do with the pig poo, which would almost certainly be worse than anything anybody had ever done with it before.

"And there's another thing you haven't thought of," said Mom.

"What's that?" asked Alice.

"How much I like bacon!" said Mom. "I'd go out there and finish it off one day with the woodchopper, I know I would. I wouldn't be able to help myself!"

"You *wouldn't!*" said Alice.

"Just try me," said her mother darkly.

Oliver had had just about enough of this. Alice was much too young and irresponsible to have a pet, and she seemed to have avoided saying the word *animal,* which was rather annoying, and anyway it was time somebody paid some attention to him. He started to tell them all about what *he* had done at school that day. His class was studying dinosaurs, and Oliver had made a really nice model triceratops, a *proper* triceratops, and his teacher had said it was absolutely wonderful and had put it out on display.

"Marvelous!" said Mom. "Well done!"

"A triceratops," said Oliver again, looking sniffily at Alice. "A difficult word to say."

"Triceratops," said Alice, sounding bored. It wasn't a difficult word at all; it never tried to be anything it wasn't.

3

Cake Cake

Alice's birthday was in July, and her parents had started to whisper secret things to each other. She knew they were planning her cake.

The Singer children never had ordinary birthday cakes. Mom and Dad got together and made them a special cake that would remind them in some way of the year that had just finished. Mom baked the cake and Dad did the frosting. They planned it all very carefully. You didn't get a special cake when you turned one. Mom said there was no point, because all you did until then was drink milk and soil diapers, and she wasn't making a diaper cake, not for anybody.

So Rosie, who was three, had had two cakes by now. When she was two, she had a fire cake, in memory of the time she set fire to the kitchen. When she was three, she had a brick cake. Alice didn't understand this at first.

"Why a brick?" she asked, puzzled. "Rosie never does any building. She knocks things down."

"In memory of all the things she's thrown at people this year," said Dad.

"But she hasn't thrown a brick at anyone!" said Oliver, frowning at the brick cake, almost as if he was about to tell his parents to throw it away and make a proper one.

"She would have if she had had one," said Dad.

"And I wanted to do something that fit one of our cake pans for once," said Mom. "That fire cake took me weeks. I'd never had a cake that I was *supposed* to burn before."

Oliver's cakes had always been rather complicated: a train cake, a Lego cake, an airplane cake, a stegosaurus cake. When he had the airplane cake, the year he was seven, he had taken one look at it and complained that the wings weren't pointing the right way and the nose wasn't done properly. Mom and Dad gave each other a long, dark look when they heard this, and the next year, when Oliver was eight, he got a cake cake. An ordinary everyday cake, round, with fruit filling in the middle and pink frosting on top that had "HAPPY BIRTHDAY OLIVER" written on it in white squiggles.

"What's that?" Oliver said, looking at the cake in horror. "It's just a cake! It's not in memory of anything!"

"Oh yes it is," said Mom. "It's in memory of your last birthday, when you were so rude about the airplane cake we worked so hard on."

Oliver went pink, and said nothing.

Alice had had a penguin cake, after Polly, who had been her favorite stuffed animal when she was little. Then, the summer when she was always rushing out into the garden to wave at the hot air balloons passing over the house, she got a balloon cake. The year she was crazy about Sesame Street brought a Big Bird cake, which was a bit too yellow for most people's taste. Then when she was five, she got a Chutes and Ladders cake, which was easy for Mom because it was just square-shaped, but took Dad hours and hours with the frosting, making the chutes and ladders and numbers.

When she was six, she got a bandaged-hand cake in memory of the time she'd fallen off the swing at the park and hurt her wrist and had to go to hospital to have it all bandaged up. That one was hard for Mom, because it was a very peculiar shape, but easy for Dad because it was all just pink hand and white bandage. And last year she'd had an angel cake to commemorate her first-ever speaking part in the Nativity Play.

This year she had no idea what kind of cake she would get. She didn't know what presents to expect either. She hadn't forgotten about the little pig, and she talked about it sadly from time to time, and drew lots of pictures of pigs and left them around the house, but she didn't really believe it would make any difference.

The family was having dinner, two days before Alice's birthday, when Mom said: "Now, Alice, your birthday is on Tuesday, but you're not having

your party until Saturday. When do you want your cake and your presents?"

This was a difficult question. Of course Alice wanted something special to happen on her *actual* birthday. But then none of her friends would see her cake because they wouldn't be coming until Saturday, which was a very long time afterwards.

"I don't know," Alice said.

"Tell you what," said Dad. "Everyone who comes to the party will bring a present, so you'll have lots of them to open on Saturday anyway, and a birthday dinner with all your favorite treats. So why don't you have *our* things on Tuesday? To make it a bit special, you could invite just one friend."

"But then the others won't see the cake," said Alice. "It'll be all eaten up by Saturday."

"They can see the photographs," said Mom. "You know your father always takes about a hundred photographs of the cake before anyone's allowed to touch it."

This was true.

"All right, then," said Alice. "I'll ask Sophie Adams."

"Is this really necessary?" asked Oliver.

"Good," said Dad. "I like Sophie. She makes me laugh."

Alice was glad that there would be at least one friend there to see her cake.

"But I wish I knew what my cake's going to be," she said. "I just can't think of anything special enough that's happened this year."

"Perhaps it will be a nothing cake, then," said Mom. "For the year you did nothing."

"A nothing cake?" said Alice. It sounded terrible.

"Yes," said Mom. "It means a cake where your Dad and I have to do nothing. We give you the flour and eggs and sugar and frosting, and you make it yourself."

Her parents began to laugh. Alice looked at them very hard to make sure they were only joking.

"I expect you will get some sort of *animal* cake," said Oliver. "All I can remember about you this year is how you kept on saying that word wrong."

"Better than getting a cake cake!" Alice said sharply, and Oliver glared at her.

"Cake cake!" shouted Rosie, who enjoyed a fight, and always knew exactly what to say to make things worse.

"That's quite enough about cakes until Tuesday," said Mom. "You'll all drive me crazy."

4

Pink Sparkly Sugar

When Alice got home from school on Tuesday, she wasn't allowed to go into the back yard. She shuddered with excitement, wondering what it was that was out there that she wasn't allowed to see.

"Am *I* allowed to go into the yard, Mr. Singer?" asked Alice's friend Sophie.

"No," said Dad.

"I wouldn't tell Alice what it is!" said Sophie.

"You would!" said Dad.

"I bet you one hundred million dollars I wouldn't!" said Sophie.

"I bet you one hundred million dollars with pink sparkly sugar on top that you would!" said Dad.

"I bet you don't even have any pink sparkly sugar!" said Sophie.

Alice's father smiled. "Maybe I do and maybe I don't, but nobody is allowed in that yard except me. And Alice's mother, when she gets home."

Oliver would almost certainly have argued about this if he had been there, but he had chess club after school on Tuesdays and wouldn't be back until quarter to five. Rosie would definitely have argued about it. In fact, if Rosie wasn't allowed out in the yard, Alice couldn't understand why she wasn't out there already, or else standing in the kitchen trying to break the door down.

"Where's Rosie?" she said.

"Oh, that was easy," said Dad. "I told her she wasn't allowed to play in her bedroom while Sophie was here, so of course she's been up there ever since she got back from daycare."

At last Oliver and Mom got back, and everything was ready, and Alice and Sophie and Rosie were called downstairs. They had all been together in Oliver's room, which faced the yard, desperately

peering out of the window and trying to figure out what it was that they weren't supposed to see.

It all looked just the same; the grass, the shed, the earthy spot where Dad had tried to grow lettuce last year but the snails had eaten it, and Oliver's rabbit in its hutch. Alice tried hard not to wish too much for a pig in case she was disappointed, but you never could tell. Maybe, just maybe, Mom had called the farm and said: "My little girl came here on a school visit a couple of weeks ago, and she made such friends with this little pig, and we wondered if perhaps we might buy it from you?" And maybe the people at the farm had said: "Oh yes, I remember your little girl! She had long curly brown hair, and the pig fell in love with her and followed her everywhere. Of course she must have it!"

They raced downstairs and into the kitchen, and there was Alice's cake, sitting in the middle of the table with a tea towel covering it. Six presents were laid out in a row behind.

"Are we all here?" said Dad. "Are we all ready?"

"Yes!" breathed Alice.

Dad made a noise like someone blowing a fanfare on a trumpet and whipped back the tea towel with a great flourish, and there was Alice's eighth birthday cake.

It was a pig cake.

It had a little fat body and a snouty sniffing pig face with a snubby pig nose; it had a curly tail, and one of its back legs wasn't as long as the other. It was a pig that would limp. It was her pig.

"Oooooh!" said Alice, stepping forward. "Oh, it's perfect!"

"I want that!" said Rosie, preparing to make a charge. This was what Rosie always said whenever she saw anything new. Her mother picked her up very quickly.

"What's all that glittery stuff on its feet?" asked Sophie, going up to the table to look at the pig more closely. The pig did indeed have its hooves outlined in shiny pink stuff.

"Pink sparkly sugar!" said Dad. "I told you I had some, Sophie. Now you owe me one hundred million dollars."

"I want that!" screamed Rosie, kicking her legs frantically and reaching out for the cake.

"But there aren't any candles!" said Sophie.

"We aren't allowed to have candles in it until Dad's taken the photographs," Alice said.

She was starting to get a bad feeling. She was feeling that if her parents had bought her a pig for her birthday, then they wouldn't have made her a pig cake as well. That would be just too much pig for one day. She knew, now, quite certainly, that whatever it was that was outside in the yard, it wasn't going to be a pig. And what else could there be in the *yard* that anyone would want? And how was she going to stop herself from looking disappointed and making Mom and Dad feel bad?

Dad began to take the photographs. He took a photo of Alice with the pig cake, one of Alice and Sophie with the pig cake, and one of Oliver standing behind Alice, Sophie, and the pig cake and looking down at them in a sniffy sort of way. He took a photo of Rosie trying to kick Alice, and a photo of Rosie trying to punch Oliver, and one of

Mom smiling nervously at the pig cake. It was not possible to get a photo of Rosie with the pig cake because the pig cake would not have survived their being so close together.

"Time to put the candles in now," said Mom, who had eight candles in their holders ready to be stuck into the top of the cake.

Dad looked miserable. He always hated this moment because it meant the end of his perfect frosting. The candle-holders made cracks in it, and then as soon as the candles were blown out, people started to eat the cake and it was gone forever.

"Come on now, be brave," said Mom to Dad. She stuck the eight candles in the pig, two in its head, two in its middle, three in its legs, and one down by its curly tail, and lit them. Then Mom and Dad and Sophie sang "Happy Birthday." Oliver, who was suspicious of singing, just moved his lips a little bit, and Rosie was busy kicking the fridge. Alice took a deep breath and blew as hard as she could. The candles were quite a distance from each other, and for a moment she thought she wouldn't have enough puff left for the last one, the one closest to the pig's curly tail. But it faded and died with the very last second of her breath.

"Well done, Alice," said her mother.

"I suppose you're all going to want to eat it now!" said Dad.

"Yes!" said Sophie gleefully. They took out the candle-holders, and Mom cut the cake up into slices. Dad pretended not to look. Everybody had a piece of cake. There was chicken and French fries for later, but when it was a birthday you were allowed to have cake first.

Sophie ate up half of her piece and then said: "Isn't it time for the presents now?"

Sophie had never been to a Singer birthday dinner before, and she was getting worried. It seemed that you could never be quite sure what would come next. Things all happened in the wrong order. It was quite possible that Alice's father wouldn't let her open the presents until he'd taken photographs of those too, and as for the chicken, it might be for breakfast tomorrow morning, and Sophie would have gone home by then.

"Presents!" said Mom. "Come on, then, Alice."

"Mine's the one with the turtles on the wrapping paper," said Sophie.

Alice knew this already, because Sophie had been carrying it around all day at school. She looked at the presents and gave a deep sigh. Half of her was longing to tear open the paper, and half of her wanted them to stay there where they were so that she'd still have all those surprises left.

She started off with Oliver's present because Oliver's presents weren't usually very exciting. It was long and thin and very neatly wrapped and taped down.

It was a ruler.

"Thank you, Oliver," Alice said.

"I thought you needed some help to draw straight lines properly, Alice," said Oliver.

"Thank you, Oliver," she said again. "I'm sure I'll have a lot of fun with it."

Oliver nodded.

Next she opened Rosie's present, which she knew Mom and Dad had bought because Rosie didn't have any money. It was a yo-yo.

"I want that," said Rosie.

Sophie had bought her a little Lego pirate island set with a treasure chest full of silver coins, a parrot, and a monkey. That left the three presents from Mom and Dad. The smallest present was a glitter paint set. The middle-sized present was a game called Manic Marbles where you had to twist and turn wheels with marble-sized holes in them, and try to collect more marbles than anybody else. Rosie wanted that so much that she had to be taken out of the room for five minutes to quiet down. And the biggest present was a toy computer that talked and played games with you and gave you puzzles to solve.

Except that it wasn't really the biggest present. There was still something out in the backyard.

5

Grotbucket

"Can we go outside now, Mrs. Singer?" asked Sophie. "Please please please?"

"Yes, I think it's time," said Mom.

Sophie and Rosie raced to the back door.

"No, wait! Alice must go first," said Mom. They all turned around and looked at Alice.

Alice didn't move. Her feet felt stuck. She couldn't go outside. She couldn't! As long as she stayed inside, there was still the faintest chance of the pig. The moment she went out and saw the thing that was there which was not a pig, then the pig was gone forever. But she could not possibly explain this to anybody, so she pulled herself together and walked out of the back door, staring straight ahead and not allowing anybody to catch her eye.

On the patio was a box. It was long and low, and made of pale, pale brown wood like a lollipop stick. It was pointing away from Alice.

"Go around and look!" said Dad.

Everyone was waiting for her. Alice walked around to the front of the box, and saw that it wasn't a box at all. It was a hutch, like Oliver's rabbit hutch. They had gotten her a rabbit. Her heart lurched with disappointment. It wasn't that she didn't like rabbits. It wasn't that she had really expected a pig. It was just that whatever you got for your birthday, you didn't want it to be something Oliver had already. You wanted something Oliver *didn't* have. She had thought her parents would have understood that.

Sophie ran up to the hutch, knelt down in front of it, and peered through the wire netting.

"A rabbit!" she squealed. "I can see it. It's so sweet. Look!"

Alice knew that Sophie was doing all the things she was supposed to be doing herself.

"No, it's not a rabbit," said Mom.

Alice turned around in surprise. Not a rabbit?

"It's a guinea pig!" said Mom. "It's the nearest thing to a real pig we could manage, Alice. We even tried to find one with a limp, but they were all sold out."

A guinea pig. Alice stepped forward slowly, squatted down, and took a good look.

Her guinea pig stared back at her.

It was adorable.

It was the color of golden honey. Its tiny pink nose twitched furiously as it blinked at Alice through the front of the cage. It was soft and furry and cuddly and it was absolutely nothing like a rabbit whatsoever. Rabbits were floppy and lollopy, but the guinea pig was a warm, firm capsule shape with no loose skin anywhere. And it was *hers*.

"Is it a boy or a girl?" she asked. "What's its name?"

"He's a boy," said Mom. "And he doesn't have a name yet. That's up to you. He's your guinea pig."

Alice gulped. She'd chosen names for toys before, but never for anything alive.

"Let's get him out," said Mom. "He can come into the kitchen. I don't want him to make a habit of it, but today's special. Go on, Alice, just undo the hook there."

Alice lifted the hook up and slowly opened the front of the cage. She was a bit nervous about picking the guinea pig up. It would probably be all right, but he *might* bite her, or he *might* pee all over her, and he *might* be so frightened of her that he would run screaming to the back of the cage, and Oliver would say the most horrible things.

But when she reached in, cupped her hands gently under the guinea pig's tummy, and drew him out, he made no effort to fight her, but just gazed up at her, all hopeful and trusting with his little quivery nose.

"I want that!" screamed Rosie, who had been busy inside opening all Alice's glitter paints and tipping them onto the floor in the bathroom. She had only just noticed the guinea pig for the first time. The guinea pig gave a fearful shudder at the sight and sound of Rosie. Alice could feel him trembling.

"Take her away!" Alice said. "She's frightening him."

"Rosie, be quiet, or you're going up to your room this minute!" said Mom.

Rosie opened her mouth, ready to scream.

"I mean it," said Mom. "Straight up to bed!"

Rosie stuck her lip out and stalked off down the backyard to sulk. "Don't want that silly pig!" she shouted over her shoulder.

"Good," said Alice, and went indoors, carrying the guinea pig as carefully as if he were eggs or glass and would break into a thousand pieces if dropped. She sat at the table with the guinea pig on her lap. After a few seconds he stopped shaking and sat still. She stroked him softly.

"He smells so nice," she said. The guinea pig smelled of warm dry sawdust. A curling-up snoozy home sort of smell.

"You'll have to clean his cage out every week," said Dad. "Or he won't smell nice for long."

"What are you going to call him?" asked Sophie, leaning over and touching the guinea pig's ear, which set him off quivering again.

"I hope you're going to give him a proper name, Alice," said Oliver sternly. Oliver's rabbit was called Peter. He was a sniffy rabbit, and never any fun. He was very much like Oliver. "This is a real live *animal*, not a toy. He must have a sensible name."

"But names can be anything," said Alice. "They don't have to be proper. I can call him *any- thing I want*." A delicious feeling ran through her as she realized that this was true.

"No, no, no," said Oliver.

"Yes, yes, yes," said Alice. "Anything I want. I can call him Dribblesnurge!"

"You can't!" Oliver was starting to go pink, the way he did when he was angry.

"Or Snurfboggit! Or Lurgerburger!"

"No!" shouted Oliver.

"Or Slimebungle! Or Ponglebottom!" said Alice.

Sophie was laughing so much by now that she fell off her chair and lay, shaking with giggles, on the floor.

"NO!" shouted Oliver.

The guinea pig huddled more closely up to Alice for protection.

"Or what about Grotbucket?" said Alice dreamily.

"Mom," said Oliver, "tell her she's not allowed!"

"I'm afraid I can't do that, Oliver. He is Alice's guinea pig, after all. She has the right to call him anything she likes, except for really rude words."

"But she said Grotbucket. That's rude!"

"Oh, I don't think so," said Dad. "It's rather an interesting name. There's nothing wrong with buckets that I know of, and 'grot' doesn't mean anything at all."

"It must be rude," said Oliver. "You know it is!"

"Maybe in guinea pig language it means 'Field of pleasant summer flowers dancing in the breeze," said Mom, half-choking with giggles. "You never can tell."

Dad was laughing his head off, and Sophie was still rolling around on the floor.

Oliver turned toward Alice, tense and furious.

"Alice," he said, "you are not to call that guinea pig Grotbucket or any silly name like that. Do you understand me?"

Alice gazed into the distance. A wonderful, wonderful idea was forming itself in her mind.

"All right," she said. "I won't."

Oliver looked at her sternly. Slowly, people stopped laughing.

"Really not?"

"Really," said Alice. She lifted the little guinea pig up so that everybody could see him. "I've decided what his name is going to be." Everybody went quiet. Even Rosie, who had crept in through the back door to see what all the laughing was, said not a word.

"His name is Aminal." said Alice.

"Aminal!" shouted Rosie.

"You can't call him *Animal*," said Oliver.

"I'm not going to. His name is *Aminal!*"

"But that's not a word!"

"It doesn't matter. It's his name!"

"Mom, tell her she can't call him *Animal*. I mean, she can't call it that."

"It's *Aminal,* Oliver," said Alice. "You really must learn to say it properly."

"But nobody could say it properly because it's not the right way!"

"Rosie can," said Alice. "I can. Aminal, Aminal, Aminal! Hello, Aminal!" She tickled the guinea pig under the chin. She could feel his heart beating as he pressed against her.

"Well, there we are, then," said Mom. "You seem to have a name, little guy. Welcome to the family, Animal. I mean Aminal. Oh, dear. This isn't going to be as easy as I thought. We'll have to practice."

"I'm not going to call him by that word," said Oliver.

Alice smiled sweetly at him. "You should always call things by their proper names, Oliver. It's not such a difficult word."

Mom and Dad both gave her an enormous wink at the same time.

"I hate you all!" shouted Oliver, running out of the room and into the bathroom and slamming the door.

There was a shout and the sound of Oliver falling over.

"Oliver?" said Dad. "What's happened?"

Rosie, who knew what had happened, tiptoed silently out of the back door and went to hide in her special hiding place at the back of the yard.

Oliver opened the bathroom door and stumbled out. "There was slippery stuff on the floor and I fell!" he howled.

Alice, Mom and Dad, and Sophie and the guinea pig all turned around and looked at him.

Oliver was covered from head to toe with glitter paint. His hair was clogged with purple glitter paint. Red glitter paint dripped down his face like sparkling blood. His clean white T-shirt was soaked with patches of blue, green, and yellow. His clean brown shirt and his thin white arms twinkled orange.

"Rosie!" he roared.

"Now I really am sending her to her room," said Mom. "Oh, poor Oliver. Never mind, I'm sure it'll all wash out. I'm sorry about your

paints, Alice. It wasn't your fault. I'll get you another set tomorrow."

"Oh, thank you," said Alice, gazing at her brother in rapture. "But don't be angry with Rosie. Please don't."

Oliver covered with glitter paint was the funniest thing she had ever seen in her life, though she didn't dare laugh out loud. On her lap, her very own guinea pig put his front paws on the edge of the kitchen table for a look around. She had a whole pile of presents she had hardly even looked at yet. She was too happy to want Rosie to be sent upstairs in disgrace, which would cast a huge black shadow over the rest of her birthday. Rosie's absence was sometimes as powerful a force as Rosie herself. Alice was never quite sure how she did this.

"Well, all right," said Mom. "If you say so — as it's your birthday. I've never known a day like it." She looked around. Oliver stood in the middle of the room shaking his fists and dripping rainbows of paint onto the floor. Sophie was still lying on the floor, waving her legs in the air. Rosie was in

the yard hiding behind the shed, with handfuls of earth ready to hurl at anyone reckless enough to try and bring her back inside.

And, in the middle of the kitchen table, there was a half-eaten pig cake, with a small honey-colored guinea pig sitting next to it and nibbling large pieces out of its curly tail. The world had gone completely crazy.

"Happy birthday, Alice," Mom said. "And now, I think it's time for that chicken."